Arthur's Adventure in the Abandoned House

Also by Fernando Krahn

Robot-bot-bot
Catch That Cat!
The Mystery of the Giant Footprints
Who's Seen the Scissors?
April Fools

Arthur's Adventure in the Abandoned House

by Fernando Krahn

E. P. Dutton New York

Library of Congress Cataloging in Publication Data

Krahn, Fernando.
Arthur's adventure in the abandoned house.

Summary: When he stops to explore an abandoned house, Arthur stumbles into a dangerous adventure which he handles with calm resourcefulness and a bit of luck.
[1. Adventure stories. 2. Stories without words]
1. Title.
PZ7.K8585Ar 1981 [E] 80-22249
ISBN 0-525-25945-7 AACR1

Published in the United States by E. P. Dutton, Inc., New York

Published simultaneously in Canada by Clarke, Irwin & Company Limited, Toronto and Vancouver

Editor: Ann Troy Designer: Emily Sper

Printed in the U.S.A.
10 9 8 7 6 5 4 3 2

HELP!! WE ARE PRISONERS
IN THE ABANDONED HOUSE.
ARTHUR

HELP!!
ARTHUR